The Ma

She Found Everyone Love—Except Herself

Quiet Hearts of Lancaster

Tessa Marie Vaughn

Thank you for reading this special collection. I hope you enjoy every story inside.

Scan to explore more stories & exclusive updates!

Table of Contents

The Matchmaker's Regret

Description

Esther Whitlow has made a quiet life from helping others find the love she's never dared to seek herself. As Willow's End's most trusted matchmaker, she's guided dozens of couples into lasting happiness—carefully avoiding the risk of opening her own heart. When a grieving widower arrives in town with three children and a hesitant request for help, Esther agrees to assist him the only way she knows how: by finding him a new wife.

Caleb Martin never expected to fall into Esther's world so easily. Her calm voice soothes his guilt. Her gentle presence stirs feelings he thought long buried. But as Esther introduces him to women who check every box, Caleb begins to wonder if what he truly needs can't be written down in a notebook.

With each stolen glance and shared moment, the line between matchmaker and match begins to blur. And Esther, who has spent her life stepping aside for the sake of others, must finally choose: protect her heart—or give it away.

Can two people built from loss and self-denial find the courage to accept the kind of love neither dared to ask for?

What if the match you've been looking for... is the one you never meant to make?

Chapter 1: A Lonely Talent

Esther

The last guest had just left, her boots clicking against the wooden floor of the fellowship hall, when Esther closed the door behind her and leaned her back against it. The quiet fell fast and heavy. The laughter, the chatter, the congratulations—all faded into the hush of her own breath and the echo of memories she didn't invite.

The match had gone well. Better than expected, really. Ruth and Levi had stood beneath the hand-carved arch that Esther's uncle made for her very first match years ago, and they'd looked at each other like no one else existed. The parents beamed. The church sisters sniffled into handkerchiefs. Someone had even brought Esther a peach pie.

Twenty-seven successful matches. Twenty-seven couples who had her to thank for the way their hands now fit so perfectly together.

She walked slowly through the hall, trailing her fingers along the edge of the long table still scattered with cups and crumbs. The scent of sweet cider lingered in the air, mingling with the wax from the candles she'd lit before the ceremony. It was warm here. Safe. Full of other people's joy.

Her heels clicked softly as she gathered stray napkins and set the folding chairs back in place. She could've asked someone to help clean up, but she never did. She liked the stillness afterward—the moment when the work was done and all the emotions had passed through the walls like a breeze.

She liked it, except when she didn't.

Esther straightened a chair that didn't need straightening, then stopped, palms resting on the cold metal back. A thin film of something gathered in her throat, that familiar tightness she'd long since stopped fighting. She closed her eyes.

She could still see their faces—every one of the brides and grooms she'd matched. The way their eyes lit up during that first knowing glance, the way nervousness turned to certainty in small, unspoken moments. She could even recall the questions she'd asked, how she'd coaxed stories out of reluctant hearts until they revealed their true shape.

But she could never seem to shape her own.

***

The sky had darkened by the time she locked the hall and walked the short path home. Her boots kicked up dust as she passed the quiet storefronts, the lamplight flickering in windows already closed for the night. She tucked her shawl closer to her shoulders—not so much against the cold as the loneliness that wrapped around her like fog.

Home was a narrow cottage tucked behind the bakery. Ivy crept up the side wall, the window box beneath her kitchen window now bare with the coming winter. She stepped inside and shut the door gently, as if any loud sound might echo too much in the stillness.

The kettle was already set for tea. Habit. She lit the stove and sat in the rocking chair beside the hearth, hands clasped in her lap.

She wasn't unattractive. She knew that. People had said it enough times that she'd learned to believe them, even if the mirror sometimes told a different story. She was thoughtful. Capable. Trusted. But something inside her had always recoiled at the idea of putting herself forward. It felt like taking instead of giving—like asking for something when her whole life had been about offering.

A soft knock at the door startled her. She blinked, unsure whether she'd imagined it. Then came another.

She rose slowly, heart tapping faster against her ribs.

When she opened the door, it was Mrs. Baum standing there, cheeks pink from the wind and gray curls tucked beneath her bonnet.

"Forgive the hour," the older woman said gently. "I just came from the station. We've had a new arrival."

Esther blinked. "A new arrival?"

Mrs. Baum stepped closer. “A man. Widower. Three young children. He’s come to stay at the Miller cottage while he gets settled. He’s... he’s in need of help.”

Esther tilted her head. “What kind of help?”

Mrs. Baum’s voice dropped. “He’s looking for a wife, Esther.”

The words landed like a stone at the bottom of her stomach. The kettle began to whistle behind her.

“He asked for me?” she asked quietly.

Mrs. Baum smiled. “No, dear. I offered. Told him if anyone could help him find the right soul, it would be you.”

There was no flattery in her tone. Just plain fact. The kind that carried weight in a place like theirs.

Esther nodded slowly. “Of course. I’ll stop by tomorrow.”

“Thank you, dear.” Mrs. Baum touched her hand briefly before turning to go.

Esther stood in the doorway long after the woman had disappeared into the night. The kettle screamed in the kitchen, but she didn’t move.

She had known the feeling before—that quiet tremble of something about to shift. A tremor before the storm. But this felt different. It wasn’t fear. Or even excitement.

It was the sharp edge of longing pressing just beneath the skin.

She turned back inside and let the kettle cry a moment longer.

***

She dreamt of snow that night. Not the biting kind—soft flakes falling on a quiet hill. There were small footsteps. A child's laugh. And then a man's voice—warm, low, unfamiliar—calling her name.

She woke with the weight of it still in her chest.

***

Morning came with clouded skies and a trace of frost on the glass. Esther wrapped her shawl tighter as she walked toward the Miller cottage, a modest home with weathered shutters and a pale blue door.

Toys were scattered across the porch. A worn tricycle. A cloth rabbit missing one ear.

She hesitated at the gate, heart fluttering with something she couldn't quite name.

A child appeared in the window—wide-eyed, curious, brown curls bouncing as she called out behind her. Esther heard the thump of hurried footsteps, the creak of a door swinging open.

And then there he was.

Caleb Martin.

Taller than she expected. Hair dark as winter bark. Eyes... not sad, exactly. But worn. Like a man who'd walked far and no longer knew what to carry.

"Miss Esther?" he asked, voice hesitant.

She nodded, clearing her throat. "Mrs. Baum said you might need help."

His smile was faint, like something remembered more than felt. "I do. But only if you've the time."

"I always have time," she said, though she wasn't sure it was true anymore.

He stepped aside to let her in, and she caught the scent of woodsmoke and cinnamon and something else—*grief*, maybe, made invisible but still clinging to the corners of the room.

The children peeked from behind the stair railing. Three pairs of cautious eyes. A boy with a serious face. A girl with braids too long for her small frame. And the youngest, clutching the earless rabbit.

"I'm hoping to give them some kind of home," Caleb said quietly, following her gaze.

Esther didn't answer right away. Her eyes moved across the small living room, the books on the mantel, the picture frame turned backward on the shelf.

"You've come to the right place for that," she said softly. "We take care of each other here."

His shoulders eased just slightly. “That’s what I’m hoping.”

She turned to look at him fully then. There was kindness in his face. And pain. And a stillness that felt too familiar.

She took a deep breath.

“Tell me,” she said, folding her hands, “what kind of woman are you looking for?”

Chapter 2: A New Arrival

Caleb

The wind picked up just as Caleb stepped off the train platform, lifting his coat and rattling the last brittle leaves from the maples lining the main street. He kept one hand firm on his youngest daughter's shoulder as she clung to her rabbit—the one she wouldn't sleep without. Lila hadn't spoken since they boarded the train two days ago, not even when he bought her favorite cinnamon twist at the station bakery.

Ben trudged behind him, quiet and stiff, eleven going on thirty. And Maggie—bright, too-aware Maggie—gripped his other hand like she was still trying to be brave for everyone else.

The station attendant had pointed them toward the Miller cottage at the edge of town. Caleb hadn't really heard the directions. He was too busy counting his children in his head—*three hearts to guard, three lives to rebuild, three fragile reasons to keep going.*

They passed a signpost carved with a painted arrow: *Welcome to Willow's End.*

It sounded like the last line in a story. A town that tucked you in for the winter and didn't ask too many questions.

He hoped that part was true.

***

The Miller cottage looked exactly as it had in the old photos—the ones Anna once tucked into a letter from her aunt's house, years ago. She'd described it as small and kind. The kind of home where bread cooled on the windowsill and children left their boots by the door.

He'd forgotten that letter until now. And he wished he hadn't remembered it.

Inside, the air was cold but clean. Someone had swept the floors and dusted the mantle. No dishes, no linens—just walls and space and silence. The kind that wrapped around you when everyone else was already gone.

Lila wandered toward the hearth and sat cross-legged on the rug without a word. Maggie went straight to the kitchen, inspecting cabinets like she could make them fill by staring hard enough. Ben stood in the doorway like he might still turn around and leave.

Caleb exhaled slowly and set the last bag down near the stairs. His shoulder ached from the weight of carrying too much alone.

Later that night, after the children had been bathed and tucked into borrowed blankets, he sat in the armchair by the front window. He didn't light the lamp. The dark was quieter.

He stared out at the trees lining the path and wondered if he'd made a mistake. If starting over was just a different kind of running.

The sound of footsteps outside startled him. He leaned toward the window, but saw only shadows. Then the soft knock came—just once. And then again.

He opened the door to find an older woman with silver curls beneath a shawl and sharp, steady eyes.

"I'm Mrs. Baum," she said. "I tend the church records and the town's welcome basket—though I've left it by your gate."

He glanced behind her. A wicker basket waited beside the fence—blankets, jars, a loaf of something wrapped in wax paper.

"You've brought more than welcome," he murmured.

She smiled gently. "You've brought more than most. We heard about your loss. We don't ask questions here. But we offer help—when it's wanted."

He nodded, his throat tightening. "Thank you."

She paused, studying him.

"I took the liberty of suggesting someone to help you. A woman named Esther. She's... well. She's the one you see when you need help finding your way again."

"I'm not sure I'm ready for that."

"No one ever is," she said softly. "But time won't wait for your readiness, Mr. Martin."

She turned before he could respond, disappearing into the cold.

He shut the door and leaned against it, closing his eyes.

Esther.

He repeated the name in his mind, unsure why it settled into his bones like a note played low on a cello.

***

The next morning, the house was filled with the scent of oats and old wood. Maggie had managed to mix something from the dry goods in the welcome basket. Lila sat on the floor with her doll, whispering to no one he could see. Ben had gone outside before breakfast and hadn't said where.

Caleb stood at the window, watching his son rake patterns into the frost-dusted dirt with the heel of his boot. He didn't call him back inside. He knew what it was like to need the air more than the warmth.

A knock came just before ten. Not sharp, not hesitant—measured.

He opened the door and saw her.

She stood with her shawl tucked neatly, the cold pinking her cheeks. Her hands were clasped in front of her, posture straight, expression composed. But her eyes... they were darker than he expected. Not in color, but in depth.

"I'm Esther," she said softly. "Mrs. Baum may have mentioned me."

He nodded, stepping back. "She did."

She didn't move to enter until he gestured. Her shoes were practical. Her voice, quiet but certain. She walked into the room like someone who already knew how to navigate silence.

"Thank you for coming," he said.

"I don't do this as business," she replied. "I help because it's needed."

"Still," he said, "I appreciate it."

Esther looked around without judgment. Her gaze landed on the unlit hearth, the pile of folded blankets, the children's shoes by the stairs.

"I don't match people the way some imagine," she added, turning to him. "It's not a checklist. It's not a promise. It's... *listening*. Sometimes asking questions they haven't asked themselves."

"That's fair," he said. "I'm not sure I have answers."

She tilted her head. "Then maybe that's where we begin."

He felt something shift then—not in her, but in the space between them. Like a draft catching under a closed door.

Lila wandered into the room, her rabbit dangling from one hand. She stopped when she saw Esther, eyes wide.

Esther crouched slowly to meet her gaze. "That's a very fine rabbit."

Lila nodded once, clutching it tighter.

"I had one just like him," Esther continued. "I called him Patch."

"What's his name?" Caleb asked gently.

Lila blinked. "Moss."

Esther smiled. "*Moss* is a good name. He looks brave."

Caleb watched as his daughter stepped closer without being asked. He hadn't seen that look on her face in weeks—not quite trust, but something near it.

Maggie entered next, wiping her hands on her dress. She took in Esther quickly, then offered a small, polite hello.

Esther stood again. "You have wonderful children."

"They've been through a lot."

"So have you," she said simply.

There was no pity in her voice. Just truth.

***

They sat at the small kitchen table once the children had wandered back to their games. Sunlight slanted through the window, catching on the dust floating in the air.

"I don't know what I'm looking for," Caleb said quietly. "Only that I don't want to keep walking alone."

"That's enough to start," Esther replied.

"My wife..." he paused, swallowing hard. "She died two winters ago. Fever. It was fast. I was working too much. I missed the signs."

Esther didn't speak. Didn't offer comfort too soon.

"I think the children blame me. Some days, I do too."

Her voice was softer now. "Loss has a way of leaving questions without answers. But you're here. That means something."

He nodded slowly. "I want them to have someone who... someone they can lean on. A woman who's steady. Kind. Who doesn't try too hard."

Esther's mouth curved faintly. "Trying too hard is often a sign of trying to heal something invisible."

He looked up at her then, eyes meeting hers. "Do you know many people like that?"

"I know many who *try*," she said quietly.

There was a pause—long enough that it could've turned awkward, but didn't. The quiet settled around them like snow. Not heavy. Just present.

Caleb leaned back slightly in his chair. "I don't expect miracles."

"No one does," Esther replied. "But sometimes they happen when you stop expecting."

The clock ticked from the mantle. Outside, the wind stirred the leaves into spirals.

"I'll start thinking," she said after a moment. "Listening. Watching. Asking."

He nodded again, unsure what else to say.

As she stood to leave, Lila reappeared, holding out a small green button she'd found on the floor. Esther took it gently, turned it over in her fingers, then handed it back.

"Hold onto that," she said. "Sometimes the smallest things tell the biggest stories."

Caleb walked her to the door.

"Thank you again," he said quietly.

She hesitated before replying. "We all want someone to stay. Even if we don't say it out loud."

And then she was gone.

Chapter 3: Business, Not Personal

Esther

Esther woke before the sun, the weight of yesterday still folded neatly beneath her ribs like something stored away in a drawer. She moved quietly through the house, pouring water into the kettle, lighting the stove, watching the slow bloom of flame beneath iron. The sky beyond her kitchen window was still dark, but a faint strip of lavender had begun to tug at the horizon.

She couldn't stop thinking about him.

It wasn't love. That would be absurd. She'd barely spoken to the man. But there had been something—*something* in the way his voice cracked when he spoke of his children, something in the look he gave them when he thought no one was watching. It wasn't longing exactly. Or maybe it was.

She turned from the window and pressed her hand flat against the kitchen table.

This isn't personal. It can't be. She'd been asked to help, and she would. Like always.

Her own heart had no place in it.

***

The second visit came three days later, after she'd gathered a few names from the church list and a note from the grocer about a recently returned niece. She brought a small notebook and a basket of hand pies, unsure why she'd included the latter.

The Miller cottage looked more lived-in now. A child's coat hung crookedly from the porch hook. The door stood slightly ajar. A pair of muddy boots rested beside a broom that hadn't finished its job.

She knocked gently.

Caleb opened the door with the same tired expression, but his eyes warmed when he saw her. Not lit—not yet—but warmer than before.

"Morning," he said, stepping aside. "I was hoping you'd come."

"I said I would," she replied, holding out the basket. "I brought food. And questions."

He smiled faintly. "I can't promise I've got answers, but you're welcome to try."

She followed him inside. The scent of baking and woodsmoke hung in the air. Maggie was reading aloud from a schoolbook at the table. Lila sat beneath it with a crayon and torn paper. Ben was nowhere in sight.

"I'll be in the back," Maggie said without being asked, standing and scooping Lila up in one practiced motion.

Caleb raised an eyebrow. "They've never taken to anyone so fast."

Esther shrugged lightly, settling into the same chair as last time. "Children sense who listens. Not just who speaks."

"Maybe you're better at this than I thought."

"I'm not perfect," she replied. "Just persistent."

He looked at her then, as if searching for something buried in her words. She met his gaze without flinching.

"I brought some names," she said, opening her notebook.

He watched her fingers move across the page. "Are they all... women looking for someone like me?"

She paused. "Someone kind? Wounded, but still willing? Yes."

He looked away. "I'm not sure what I have to offer."

"Don't decide that on their behalf," she said, her voice softening.

He exhaled slowly and ran a hand through his hair. "What kind of things do you usually ask?"

She flipped to a blank page. "It depends. But I start with stories—how people remember love."

His brow furrowed. "Why does that matter?"

"Because it tells me how they carry it now."

He was quiet for a moment. "I met Anna at a harvest festival. I was working the grain booth. She knocked over a basket of corn and apologized for five minutes straight."

Esther smiled without writing. "And you married her."

"Three years later. She made everything slower. I used to rush. I don't anymore."

A pause stretched between them—not uncomfortable, just unfilled.

"Do you still speak to her?" Esther asked gently.

He blinked. "She's gone."

"I mean in your heart."

Caleb looked down. "Only when I don't want the kids to see me break."

She didn't press. Instead, she jotted something small in the margin, then tucked her pencil behind her ear.

"I'd like to ask you a few things," she said. "Not to match you, but to understand the space you're making."

"All right."

"What color reminds you of safety?"

He tilted his head. "Brown. Like worn leather. Or old books."

She nodded. "Do you prefer storms or silence?"

"Silence," he answered. "But not the empty kind."

She looked up. "What do you fear more—being alone again, or letting someone in?"

The question hovered between them like dust in a sunbeam.

"I don't know yet," he whispered.

***

They walked the garden path later, a narrow trail behind the house edged with stones and tufts of stubborn winter grass. The children played inside. Caleb kept his hands in his coat pockets, and Esther kept hers clasped beneath her shawl.

"I was raised on a farm," she said quietly. "Not far from here. My parents expected I'd marry young. But I didn't. I watched others instead. Listened more than I spoke."

"That's how this started?" he asked.

"I made my first match when I was seventeen. Two neighbors who didn't know how to look each other in the eye. I saw it before they did."

Caleb smiled. "And never for yourself?"

"No," she said, watching a crow lift from the tree line. "I don't think anyone ever saw it in me."

He stopped. "That's hard to believe."

She turned to him. "You don't know me."

"I'm learning."

Her breath caught.

There was no wind, but the air felt like it moved. She didn't know what to say. She never struggled for words. But something in her wanted to retreat—to fold the moment back into a box and label it: *Not for me.*

“I’ll send word when I’ve spoken to the others,” she said, too fast.

Caleb nodded, but his eyes lingered on her longer than they should have.

She left before the silence said too much.

Chapter 4: The Search Begins

Caleb

There was something strange about hope when it arrived too soon.

It didn't rush in like fire. It crept like fog—slow, hesitant, brushing the edges of things you thought would stay broken.

Caleb felt it that morning as he poured warm water over oats, listening to the floorboards creak where Maggie walked upstairs. Lila hummed under her breath at the table, drawing tiny circles on a napkin with the corner of a spoon. Ben hadn't come down yet.

He stirred the oats absently, lost in the memory of Esther's voice—the way she had asked those quiet questions, each one gentle but unrelenting. She hadn't flinched when he spoke of Anna. She hadn't filled the silence with pity. She had simply... stayed.

That shouldn't have mattered.

She was helping him, that was all. Helping him meet someone else.

Still, he found himself standing longer at the kitchen window, watching the road that led to town.

***

Esther arrived at midday, her coat dusted with snow that hadn't been in the forecast. She carried a folder beneath her arm and her usual calm—that quiet steadiness that made noise retreat without being asked.

Caleb opened the door before she could knock.

"I was just putting on coffee," he said.

"Good," she replied, stepping inside. "It's that sort of day."

The children greeted her with a chorus of half-smiles and shy waves. Even Ben nodded. Esther settled into the chair beside the hearth, unwrapping a scarf from her neck, fingers pink from the cold.

She didn't speak right away, and neither did he. The silence was companionable, threaded with the comfort of something slowly growing roots.

"I've narrowed it down to three," she said finally, tapping the folder.

Caleb raised a brow. "Three?"

"Three women I believe you could grow beside."

He folded his hands. "Grow beside, not fall for?"

"Falling is easy," she said quietly. "Staying is the harder part."

He nodded slowly.

Esther opened the folder and slid the first sheet toward him. "Ruth Brenner. Thirty-two. Widow. No children. Teaches piano lessons and bakes every Saturday. She's practical. Patient. You'd speak the same language."

Caleb studied the page, noting the faint curve of a smile in Ruth's photo. It was warm, but distant. A smile you gave to someone else's child.

"She sounds steady," he said.

"She is."

"And the second?"

"Naomi Yates. Thirty-four. Divorced. Moved here to care for her sister. Loves gardening. Struggles with structure, but she's light. Quick to laugh. Could bring levity."

He looked down at the neat print beneath Naomi's name, then back at Esther.

"Would someone like that... want someone like me?"

"I wouldn't have listed her if I didn't believe she could see you," she said simply.

He shifted in his chair. "And the third?"

Esther hesitated—just for a second. "Sarah Holden. Thirty-five. Raised three younger siblings alone. Strong-willed. Protective. Not easily rattled."

Caleb met her gaze. "You saved her for last."

"She's not the easiest match," Esther said. "But she's honest. You wouldn't have to guess where you stood."

He tilted his head slightly. "Do you ever guess where you stand?"

The question came too raw, unfiltered.

Esther looked down at her hands. "Sometimes. But I've learned not to expect certainty from people who are still healing."

He nodded, uncertain if she meant him.

***

That afternoon, they sat together at the kitchen table. The children played quietly in the other room, and sunlight carved long, slanted lines across the floorboards.

Caleb flipped through the profiles again, his fingers lingering over Ruth's name.

"She's the safest choice," he murmured.

"She is," Esther replied.

"Would you pick her for me?"

"I don't pick. I reflect."

He looked up at her. "But what if I don't want safe?"

She didn't answer right away.

"Then say that out loud," she whispered.

He closed the folder and pushed it aside. His chest felt tight—but not with grief. It was something closer to fear... or longing. Or both.

"I'd like to meet her," he said after a pause. "Ruth."

Esther nodded, her expression unreadable. "I'll arrange something small. Simple. Maybe next Sunday after service."

"Will you be there?" he asked, not meaning to sound so eager.

She looked at him, something flickering behind her eyes. "If I'm invited."

"You are."

The silence returned—but it had changed. It wasn't soft anymore. It had edges now, the kind that scraped when you weren't careful.

***

That night, after the children had gone to bed, Caleb lingered by the window. The folder sat untouched on the table.

He should've felt something—relief, maybe. Gratitude.

But instead, his thoughts circled Esther's face... the way she'd looked when he asked if she ever guessed where she stood. How her voice had faltered—just slightly—when she said she'd come if invited.

He didn't understand it.

He didn't want to understand it.

Not yet.

Chapter 5: Little Moments

Esther

The picnic wasn't planned.

It had started with a loaf of rye she'd baked before sunrise and no one to share it with. Then a walk. Then the thought—half-formed, not yet permissioned—that maybe the children could use some sun. And maybe Caleb could too.

She hadn't meant to bring the jam. Or the dried apple slices. But somehow they ended up in her basket anyway, tucked beside two hard-boiled eggs and a napkin embroidered with her initials in faded thread.

She stopped at the gate with her fingers resting on the latch.

It was just kindness. That was all.

The wind was mild. The sky carried the soft gray light of late winter—*not quite spring, not quite done with cold.*

She knocked once. The door creaked open from the inside before her knuckles landed again.

"Miss Esther," Maggie said, surprised.

Esther smiled. "Am I too early?"

"For what?"

She lifted the basket. "To borrow your family."

The girl blinked, then grinned in a way that made something in Esther ache.

"I'll get Papa."

***

They walked to the open field just beyond the chapel grounds, where the trees thinned and the creek curled in a soft bend near the reeds. The children scattered quickly—Ben chasing Lila with exaggerated slowness, Maggie gathering stones and lining them in a row like tiny sentries.

Caleb helped Esther spread the blanket.

"You didn't have to do all this," he said, kneeling beside her.

"I wanted to," she answered. "I thought it might help to be somewhere different. Not waiting. Not planning. Just... being."

His gaze lingered on her face. "You do that a lot."

"Do what?"

"Say things no one else says out loud."

Esther looked down, brushing imaginary crumbs from her skirt. "Most people don't want to hear them."

"I do."

The words were quiet, barely touching the air. She didn't look up. She wasn't sure she could.

They sat close but not touching, legs crossed on the blanket, watching the children run themselves breathless. Caleb reached for the bread with one hand while the other rested loosely over his knee, fingers twitching now and then, like his body was still learning what to do with stillness.

"I used to think peace meant silence," he said.

"And now?"

"Now I think it might just mean space. The kind you don't have to explain."

She nodded, her throat catching slightly. "That's rare."

"I didn't know I missed it until it showed up."

Esther swallowed hard and looked out over the field.

Her mind kept drifting to a memory—one she rarely visited. A man named Simon. Tall. Gentle. Timid in a way that felt like home. They'd shared tea for three months straight one autumn, and he'd nearly asked her once. She'd seen it in his eyes, in the way his hands shook over the rim of his cup. But then his cousin arranged a match with a younger woman, and he didn't come back.

She never told anyone about that.

It felt too small to count and too large to carry.

She hadn't let herself want again after that.

Until now—*no, not want*. She couldn't call it that.

But something was beginning to stir. Something she didn't recognize but also didn't fear.

Not yet.

Lila crawled into Esther's lap without asking. Just climbed up, rabbit dangling from one arm, curls sticking to her cheeks.

Esther blinked. Her hands moved slowly, unsure, then settled gently around the small, warm frame pressing against her.

Caleb didn't say anything.

"She doesn't do that with strangers," he murmured after a while.

Esther's voice was low. "Maybe I'm not one anymore."

Maggie came and lay across the edge of the blanket, hands behind her head, eyes closed against the pale sun.

"They're happy," Caleb said.

"They feel safe," Esther corrected.

He looked at her then—*really* looked. And it was too much. She shifted slightly, breaking the gaze, smoothing Lila's hair.

"Do you think it's wrong?" she asked.

"What?"

"To get close like this. When we're supposed to be working toward something else."

Caleb's breath caught.

"I don't know," he said honestly. "But it doesn't feel wrong."

She wanted to believe him.

She wanted to stay in this moment where everything was slow and easy and possible.

But she knew better.

Tomorrow there would be introductions. There would be Ruth. There would be choice.

Today was borrowed time.

And Esther wasn't sure how to give it back.

Chapter 6: The Perfect Match on Paper

Caleb

Ruth was lovely.

She arrived precisely on time, her posture straight, her expression open but reserved. She wore a dove-gray dress that looked pressed by a careful hand and carried a small jar of homemade preserves—plum, she said. A gesture of hospitality. Or good manners. Maybe both.

Caleb stood with the front door cracked open, watching her walk up the path like she'd rehearsed it.

He hadn't told the children much—only that someone was coming by. Maggie had caught his tone, though. She always did. Ben had gone out back before the first knock, and Lila had curled up on the rug with her rabbit like she could make herself invisible.

He couldn't blame them.

He wasn't ready either.

The conversation started with warmth. Ruth had a smooth voice, the kind that settled evenly in a room—not too loud, not too soft. She spoke of her piano students, of baking with her nieces, of reading classic novels by the fire in the evening.

She asked gentle questions and gave thoughtful answers. There was nothing sharp in her tone, nothing unkind in her gaze.

He found himself nodding often. Smiling politely. Noticing the absence of discomfort—**and the absence of something else he couldn't name.**

When Lila peeked in from the hallway, Ruth turned and smiled. It was polite, encouraging. But she didn't get up. She didn't kneel. She didn't ask her name.

Esther would've.

And that thought shouldn't have come.

He forced it away and gestured to the tea.

"I've never had plum preserves," he said, unscrewing the jar.

"You'll find they go well with oat bread," she replied. "I can bring some next time, if you'd like."

Next time.

The words lingered longer than he expected.

He dipped a spoon into the jar, offering it across the table. Ruth hesitated only a moment before tasting it.

"Well?" she asked.

"It's good," he said, though he couldn't quite taste it.

***

The meeting lasted just over an hour. When Ruth stood to leave, she offered her hand.

He shook it, his fingers brushing hers with the polite pressure of formality.

“I’d be happy to visit again,” she said.

“I’d like that,” he replied, though the words sat uneasily in his mouth.

After she left, he stood at the window for a long time. The scent of her perfume lingered—floral, maybe rose. Not unpleasant. Just unfamiliar.

He didn’t feel relief or regret. Only a strange quiet, like he’d heard a song with all the right notes but couldn’t remember the melody.

***

Later that evening, after the children had gone to bed and the house had dimmed to its usual hush, he sat at the kitchen table with the half-empty jar in front of him.

He didn’t open it again.

Instead, he stared at the label. Written in perfect script: *Ruth’s Plum 3/25*.

Everything about her was neat. Clear. Proper.

Exactly what he’d said he wanted.

But every time he tried to picture Ruth in this kitchen, in this life—braiding Maggie’s hair, coaxing Ben from silence, kneeling to pick up Lila’s dropped toy—he couldn’t quite see her there.

He could only see someone else.

Someone who sat cross-legged on blankets.

Who spoke in questions.

Who didn't try too hard to be likable but somehow always was.

Esther.

And that was the problem.

He wasn't supposed to see her that way. Not now. Not while trying to build something with someone else.

He raked a hand through his hair and let his head fall into his hands.

He had asked Esther for help, and now her presence was stitched into the very seams of his household.

She had become part of the rhythm without ever demanding it.

And now he couldn't imagine the house sounding right without her in it.

***

The next morning, Caleb stood beside the stove, flipping eggs that no one had asked for. Lila had barely touched hers. Ben had left his plate half-full. Maggie picked at the corners of a slice of toast.

"I liked her dress," Maggie said quietly, glancing up. "Miss Ruth."

Caleb looked at her. "Did you?"

Maggie shrugged. "It was neat. She smiled at me, but not like she really wanted to."

He didn't answer.

Lila finally spoke, her voice small. "Where's Miss Esther?"

"She's not coming today."

"Oh."

Just that—*one syllable*. But it sank deep.

Caleb turned back to the stove, spatula trembling slightly in his grip.

He didn't know what he'd gotten himself into.

Only that he was starting to wish the matchmaker had never handed him a list in the first place.

Chapter 7: A Gentle Stirring

Esther

It was the garden that brought her back.

Not Caleb. Not the children. Not the aching silence that had stretched across the past two days like a thread she couldn't quite pull free from.

Just the garden.

Esther told herself that as her hands filled the basket with cuttings—mint, rosemary, and early shoots of lemon balm. The small bundle of lavender was for Mrs. Keene's daughter. The carrots were spoken for. The rest, she'd bring to the Miller cottage, just as she had for others, just as she always did.

It had *nothing* to do with missing the sound of Lila's shy voice or Maggie's quick wit. Nothing to do with Caleb's eyes—*darker than memory and harder to forget.*

Only the garden.

She held to that thought like a stone in her palm as she walked the path toward their home.

The back garden gate was unlatched, swaying slightly in the wind. She stepped through it without knocking, the familiar creak under her boots grounding her more than she expected.

Caleb was there, crouched beside a row of stubborn winter kale, a trowel in one hand, dirt smudged across his forearm.

He looked up as she approached, surprise flickering across his face before softening into something unreadable.

"You're here," he said.

"I'm here," she echoed, lifting the basket.

He stood slowly, brushing soil from his hands. "We missed you."

The words landed too close to where she'd hidden the part of her that *wanted* to be missed.

"I brought herbs. And carrots. Thought maybe Lila could help me wash them."

"She'd like that," he said. "So would I."

They stood in silence, wind rustling dry leaves overhead, the scent of turned earth rising faintly between them.

***

"Ruth came by again," he said after a moment.

Esther nodded, trying not to show what curled in her chest.

"She's kind," he continued. "Smart. Honest. I know you chose her carefully."

"I didn't choose," Esther said. "You asked. I offered."

He looked at her then—*really* looked—like he was searching again for something she didn't know how to give.

"She's everything I asked for," he said.

"But not everything you need?"

The question was out before she could stop it.

Caleb didn't answer. Not right away.

Instead, he reached for the watering can beside the porch and began pouring slowly into the roots of the kale. The sound of water against soil filled the space between them.

"You ever feel like you wrote a list, then met someone who wasn't on it—but still felt more right than anything else?"

Esther's hands tightened around the basket handle.

"Yes," she said.

He turned toward her, the can empty now, held loosely at his side.

"I don't know what to do with that feeling," he said.

"Neither do I."

***

They sat on the bench beneath the crabapple tree, just far enough apart to make the air between them hum.

"I was engaged once," Esther said quietly. "A long time ago."

Caleb turned to her, patient.

"His name was Simon. He was kind. Nervous. Liked numbers more than people. We had tea every Thursday."

"What happened?"

"Nothing happened. He left. Another woman. A clearer path. I didn't fight for it."

"Did it break you?"

"No," she said. "It just left something loose inside me."

They sat with that truth for a while, unjudged.

"And now?" he asked.

"Now I help other people choose. I tell myself that's enough."

"But it isn't," he said, not asking.

"No," she whispered. "It isn't."

The sun was lowering behind the church steeple, casting long shadows across the field. The children's voices echoed faintly from inside.

Caleb shifted slightly, his shoulder brushing hers—not on purpose, not fully accidental either.

She didn't move.

"I don't want to hurt Ruth," he said.

"You don't want to hurt yourself either."

"Or you," he added.

The words made her breath catch.

"I came today for the garden," she said, though they both knew better.

Caleb smiled, slow and sad. "You keep telling yourself that?"

"I have to."

He looked at her hands, still wrapped tight around the basket resting in her lap.

“You don’t,” he said.

Esther stood slowly, grounding herself before the weight of his voice could pull her back down.

“I should go,” she said.

“I know.”

She turned toward the path, but didn’t take a step.

Behind her, he stayed seated. Silent.

Waiting for her to walk away.

She did.

But each step felt like a question she couldn’t answer.

Chapter 8: The Confession That Wasn't

Caleb

The letter from Ruth arrived folded neatly in a pale blue envelope, her name scripted in even, graceful curves. Maggie brought it in from the post and set it on the table without a word. Caleb stared at it for a long time before opening it.

She thanked him for the visit. Said she enjoyed their conversations. Hoped they might walk again by the river when the thaw came.

Nothing too eager. Nothing too cold. Just polite interest.

He folded the letter once more and slid it beneath the stack of unopened bills on the counter.

It wasn't Ruth's fault.

She had done everything right—said the right things, held the right posture, offered the right kind of future.

And still, he felt like he was walking toward something without ever quite arriving.

He didn't know what he was waiting for.

Or maybe he did.

Esther hadn't returned since the day in the garden. But her absence filled the house more than her presence ever had. Her name hadn't been spoken aloud, not once, yet somehow the children kept circling around it like a story they were afraid to finish.

Lila left her drawings by the door.

Maggie offered to bake a pie with no recipe, insisting they could "just guess like Miss Esther does."

Even Ben, always quiet, had started setting an extra fork on the table without explaining himself.

Caleb said nothing. He simply gathered the signs and held them like puzzle pieces, too scattered to make sense of.

***

It was Sunday when he saw her again.

She sat two rows ahead in church, her hair tucked up in a way that exposed the curve of her neck. She didn't turn around. Didn't glance back once. But when the final hymn ended and the congregation began to rustle and rise, she stood slower than usual, as if bracing herself.

Caleb caught up to her outside, just past the oak trees that lined the walk toward the horses.

"Esther," he said.

She turned. Her face was calm, practiced. But her eyes betrayed her.

"I wasn't sure you'd come," she said.

"I wasn't sure I'd stay seated."

She gave the smallest smile–just the corners of her mouth, quickly gone.

He glanced back toward the chapel. "I've been meaning to talk."

"That's what people say when they're trying not to."

"Then I'll say it differently. I *want* to talk."

She studied him, silent.

He stepped closer. "Not about Ruth. Not about lists. About... you. About *this*."

Her arms crossed loosely in front of her—not defensive, but uncertain.

Caleb took a breath.

"I think of you when I shouldn't. When I'm with her. When I'm folding Lila's clothes or watching the kettle boil or walking past the garden. I think of you."

Esther's breath caught, just slightly. She didn't look away.

"You know this isn't right," she said softly. "I was meant to help you find someone else."

"Maybe that was a mistake."

Her voice dropped. "You can't unmake it without hurting someone."

He nodded slowly. "I know. And I've tried... I've tried to see what I'm supposed to see with Ruth. I've tried to want what makes sense."

"But you don't?"

He hesitated.

The moment cracked open.

"I don't," he admitted.

They stood together beneath the wide sky, neither touching, neither retreating.

A gust of wind swept past, stirring the edge of Esther's shawl.

"I should tell her," Caleb said. "I should end it before it becomes anything."

"You haven't kissed her?"

"No."

"Then it isn't anything yet," Esther whispered.

"But it could be," he said. "And I don't want it to be."

She blinked slowly, as if the words themselves were too much light.

"Why now?" she asked. "Why say this here, like this?"

"Because I thought I could carry it quietly. But I can't."

Esther closed her eyes for a moment. When she opened them, they glistened.

"I've spent years watching other people choose," she said. "And every time I think maybe—maybe it'll be my turn, I remind myself it's not my place."

"What if it *is*?" he asked.

She stepped back, just one pace. But it was enough.

"I don't know how to want something and not ruin it," she said.

"You're not ruining anything."

"Not yet," she whispered. "But you haven't told her."

He reached for her hand—only brushed her fingers.

"I will."

Esther nodded, slow, unsure. "Then tell me again *after*."

And she walked away. Not fast. Not fleeing.

But with the weight of everything she hadn't let herself hope for trailing behind her like a shadow.

Chapter 9: A Matchmaker's Guilt

Esther

She wrote the letter after midnight.

There was no preamble, no greeting beyond his name. Just three short paragraphs that said everything and nothing at once.

She thanked him for trusting her. For letting her walk beside him during a difficult season. She affirmed what he already knew: Ruth was a kind and capable woman. She would be good for him. For the children. For the long winters that would inevitably come.

And then she let him go.

No plea. No confession. No trace of the yearning she had folded carefully into her silence over the past weeks. The words were measured, neutral, graceful. She signed only her name.

Esther.

She sealed the envelope and stared at it for a long time. Her handwriting looked steadier than she felt. Her heart beat slowly beneath the weight of every line she hadn't written.

She lit the stove, boiled water, and watched it steam in the kettle without making tea. There was no point. She wouldn't drink it.

At sunrise, she slid the letter beneath his front door and walked away without knocking.

***

The garden felt hollow without a purpose. Her hands moved through the soil out of habit, not desire. She plucked weeds that hadn't grown yet. Trimmed herbs she wouldn't use.

The rosemary had gone brittle along the stems, its edges curling with the last bite of frost. She pressed it between her fingers, breathing in the scent that reminded her of dinners never shared, conversations never finished.

She sat on the bench beneath the apple tree and let her palms rest in her lap. The birds were loud for late March, the kind of noise that made you ache without knowing why.

In the distance, she could hear the Miller children laughing—small, uneven bursts of joy carried by the wind.

She closed her eyes.

This was what she did. She listened. She stepped in. She stepped back.

It was never supposed to be about her.

She didn't go to church that week. Or the next.

She told herself it was the weather. Or the backlog of baking orders. Or the flu spreading through the schoolhouse.

She told herself anything except the truth: that she couldn't bear to see him with someone else.

Not after what almost—but never quite—was.

Mrs. Keene stopped by to return a jar of jam and mentioned in passing that Ruth had begun walking the children home from lessons.

"She's sweet with them," the woman said. "Has a way of making them laugh without raising her voice."

Esther nodded and smiled and thanked her for the dish.

Later, she stood at her window, watching a pair of sparrows dart across the fence line, and tried not to picture Ruth's hand on Lila's back. Or Ruth sitting at the kitchen table. Or Ruth planting carrots in the garden she had once considered her own.

She hadn't realized how tightly she'd been holding onto that fantasy until she gave it away.

She hadn't realized how much it would hurt.

***

When the knock came four days later, she knew it was him.

She didn't move at first. She stood at the far end of her kitchen, apron still tied, flour dusted across the edge of her sleeve.

He knocked again. Slower this time.

She opened the door.

Caleb stood with a piece of paper in his hand. Her letter. Folded. Creased. Read and re-read.

"You shouldn't be here," she said, voice thin.

"I read this five times."

She didn't answer.

He stepped inside—not waiting for permission, not demanding it either—just crossing the threshold with the quiet certainty of someone who had already made his decision.

"You were trying to do the right thing," he said. "I know that."

"Then go," she whispered. "Let that be enough."

"I can't."

She swallowed hard, backing toward the table.

"You're supposed to be with her."

"No," he said. "I was supposed to *try*."

"And you did. And now—"

"It didn't work," he said. "Because she isn't *you*."

She looked down. "That doesn't mean I should be."

"It means you already are," he said. "You've been part of this family since the first time you walked in with that notebook. Before I even saw it happening."

Her eyes brimmed. "I wrote that letter to give you peace."

"I don't want peace if it means not having you."

"Caleb—"

"I ended it," he said quietly. "With Ruth. I told her the truth."

Esther turned away, breath catching.

"I didn't come here to ask you for anything," he said. "I just needed you to know that the choice is mine. And I already made it."

She stood with her back to him, her hands pressed flat against the counter. The light from the window hit the wall in a long, angled streak, the hour sliding slowly toward dusk.

He didn't move to close the distance.

And she didn't ask him to.

Not yet. Not quite. Not now.

But she didn't ask him to leave either.

And that, somehow, was enough.

Chapter 10: The Broken Proposal

Caleb

The wind was sharp the morning he left Ruth's doorstep without knocking.

He'd stood there too long, fingers clenched around a small bunch of violets Maggie had picked from the garden. The petals had wilted a little in his grip, crushed by the weight of what he thought he owed. What he thought he was supposed to become.

The plan had been simple. Clear the air. Be kind. Close the door gently.

But nothing about it felt simple anymore.

He didn't leave the flowers on the porch.

He took them home, and they sat on the windowsill in a chipped mug for three days—until Lila quietly moved them to the back steps and let the wind finish the rest.

***

Ruth didn't cry when he told her. She blinked slowly, her hands folded neatly in her lap. They sat in the parlor of her aunt's home, her back straight, her face calm—*too* calm.

"I appreciate your honesty," she said, not quite meeting his eyes.

"I never wanted to hurt you."

"You didn't," she replied. "Not really. I think I knew. I just hoped you didn't."

Caleb lowered his gaze. "You're a good woman."

"I know," she said gently. "And you're a good man. But we're not good together. Not in the way that matters."

There was no bitterness in her voice. Only something quieter, older—an acceptance he wasn't sure he deserved.

He stood to leave, but she stopped him with a question.

"Will you tell her?"

He hesitated.

Ruth's eyes found his now, clear and direct. "Because if you don't, she'll never believe it. Women like that... they don't expect to be chosen."

He nodded once, unable to speak.

And then he left her behind, grateful and ashamed all at once.

***

It was Ben who brought Esther back.

Not with words. Not with questions. Just with quiet insistence.

The boy appeared beside Caleb's chair at twilight, holding the envelope Esther had returned unopened. Her letter. Her goodbye. Still sealed.

"Give it back to her," Ben said. "But don't make her read it."

Caleb looked up. "Why?"

"Because she already knows. And she's scared you'll take it away."

He took the envelope from his son and felt, for the first time in weeks, that something broken might still be made whole.

***

The next morning, Caleb didn't write her another note.

He showed up.

No basket. No pretense. Just him.

He stood at her gate, unsure if he should knock. Unsure if he even had the right.

She came out anyway, her hands still damp from washing, her sleeves rolled above the elbow. She didn't look surprised. Just tired. Tired of silence. Tired of waiting for something that kept approaching but never arriving.

"I ended it," he said.

"I know."

"I didn't do it because you told me to."

"I didn't ask you to."

"I did it because I couldn't look at her and pretend it was fair."

Esther stepped off the porch but didn't come closer.

"And now?"

"Now I don't want to pretend with you either."

She crossed her arms, holding herself steady.

"I don't know how to be chosen without thinking it's a mistake."

"It's not."

"I don't know how to accept something and not feel like I stole it."

"You didn't."

He stepped forward once. Then again.

"I want to build something real," he said. "And that only happens when both people stop hiding from what they want."

Esther stared at him, lips pressed tight.

"Do you know how many times I've walked away first?" she said softly. "Because I thought it was noble? Because I didn't want to be the one who broke something?"

He nodded. "Maybe this time you don't have to walk."

"And if it still breaks?"

"Then we break together."

Something in her cracked—just enough to soften.

She took one step toward him. Then another.

"I'm not ready to say anything big," she said.

"I'm not asking for big. I'm asking for honest."

She reached into her apron pocket and pulled out the sealed letter—the one she'd sent, the one he'd tried to return. She held it out.

"Then take this. But don't open it. It was written by someone who didn't know what she was worth."

He took it slowly, held it to his chest.

"Then let's find out together," he said.

And this time, she didn't walk away.

Chapter 11: The Match Meant to Be

Esther

She didn't know what to do with peace.

It came softly, like mist rising off the fields at dawn, threading through her bones before she could name it. Not joy—not yet. Not the burst of something new. Just the quiet absence of unrest.

She had seen it happen to others. After years of building lives for them, she'd watched that shift behind the eyes—the moment when resistance gave way to hope, when people stopped bracing for disappointment.

Now it was her turn, and she hardly recognized herself.

She still woke early. Still kneaded dough before the sun cracked the sky. Still tended to the garden in silence.

But something had changed in the way she breathed. She didn't hold her breath as much. She didn't listen for footsteps that never came.

Because now\... *they came.*

Caleb stopped by often, never on a schedule, never with pretense. Sometimes he brought Lila, who wandered the herb rows with her rabbit in one hand and a piece of Esther's apron in the other. Sometimes it was Ben, who asked for quiet company more than words. Maggie came once with a sketchbook and asked to draw the willow tree behind the shed.

And sometimes, Caleb came alone.

He didn't fill the space with promises. He didn't press. He simply arrived, offering the steadiness she'd once tried to build in others but never asked for herself.

***

One afternoon, they sat on her back porch in silence for nearly an hour. The sun fell across the tips of their boots. A jar of water sat between them, sweating slightly in the warmth.

"I never told you what it was like, those first few months after Anna passed," he said.

Esther looked at him but said nothing.

Caleb kept his gaze on the distance, where the fence line met the edge of the woods.

"I didn't cry much. I just... moved. Like everything had to keep happening or I'd disappear with her."

She waited.

"I remember one night, Lila woke up screaming. I was so tired, I nearly didn't go to her. I sat at the edge of the bed, hands shaking, and I thought... maybe she'd stop on her own. Maybe I couldn't fix it."

He turned his head slowly.

"But I did go. I held her until she fell asleep again. And I whispered to myself, *You can keep showing up*."

Esther's throat tightened.

"You've kept showing up for me too," he said. "Even when you didn't mean to."

She looked away, blinking hard.

"I don't know if I'm ready to be anything more than what I am," she said.

"Good," he replied. "Because I'm not asking for more. I'm asking for now."

***

They started walking in the evenings.

No arm-in-arm strolls. No declarations under moonlight. Just two people pacing dirt paths while the air cooled and the world slowed.

Some nights they said nothing. Others, they told stories. She shared how she once broke her wrist falling off a ladder at thirteen because she'd been too proud to ask for help. He told her about his mother's recipe book, written entirely in pencil, that he still kept tucked in a drawer even though the pages were worn to smudges.

When he reached for her hand on one of those walks, he did it so slowly she almost didn't notice. But once he did, she didn't let go.

***

One Sunday morning, she returned to church.

The pew felt narrower than she remembered. The wood creaked the same, but the air around her buzzed differently. She sat beside Caleb. Maggie on the other side. Lila curled against her skirt. Ben two rows back with the other boys, pretending not to glance over.

Esther didn't sing during the hymns. But her lips moved with the words.

Afterward, people whispered. Mrs. Baum raised an eyebrow. Ruth nodded once from across the room, with something that looked a lot like grace.

And Caleb... he didn't flinch. He didn't shift away from her. He stayed close.

She hadn't realized how much that would mean until she felt it.

***

He came to her door the following Thursday with a small wooden box.

Inside were three items: a photograph of Anna, a folded drawing by Lila, and a dried sprig of rosemary.

"I don't know what people do when they decide to stop trying to make things work on paper," he said.

She touched the rosemary.

"They start from the roots," she said.

Caleb smiled. "That's what I was hoping."

She didn't kiss him.

She didn't say yes to anything.

But she opened the door wider, and this time, he stepped all the way in.

Epilogue: One Year Later

Esther

The meadow was already full when they arrived.

Blankets sprawled beneath the willow trees. Children darted between folding tables heavy with lemonade and potato salad. Someone had brought a guitar. Someone else, a crate of daffodils.

Esther stood just beyond the gathering, her basket tucked against her hip, the scent of fresh bread still warm through the cloth. Caleb was behind her, carrying the pie Maggie had insisted on making herself. Lila clutched his hand. Ben walked a few paces ahead, eyes scanning for someone he knew but wouldn't wave to. Not yet.

She watched the scene unfold like it belonged to someone else.

And maybe, for a long time, it had.

This place, this peace—it had once been the backdrop to stories she only helped others live.

Now it was hers.

She wore the simplest band. No announcement had followed. No church bells. No formal celebration. Just a quiet Sunday afternoon last fall, with the children seated close and Mrs. Baum standing beneath the crabapple tree.

Caleb had read vows written in the back of his mother's cookbook.

Esther had said hers with steady hands.

The ring had been his grandmother's—worn smooth by decades of *ordinary* devotion.

She liked that. The plainness of it. The certainty it held.

Someone called her name across the field—Ruth, smiling, walking hand in hand with a man Esther didn't recognize.

Esther raised a hand in return.

Ruth approached slowly, her face open, content. "You did it again," she said.

Esther blinked. "What do you mean?"

"Daniel," Ruth said, gesturing to the man beside her. "He showed up with a broken fence post and a basket of overripe pears. You pointed him toward the coop behind the chapel."

"I just said it needed repair," Esther murmured.

"You sent him to me."

Esther looked down, half-laughing. "I didn't mean to."

Ruth shrugged. "Sometimes you don't have to."

She touched Esther's shoulder briefly. "Thank you."

And then she walked away, Daniel at her side, already caught in the rhythm of something beginning.

***

The picnic went long into the afternoon. The sun dipped low behind the trees. Lila fell asleep on the blanket with her head in Maggie's lap. Ben sat across from Esther, chewing a piece of bread too slowly—the way he did when he didn't want to leave.

Caleb joined her at the edge of the clearing, where the garden path began.

"You see them?" he asked, nodding toward the younger couple tucked beneath one of the oaks. The boy's coat too large, the girl's hair undone by the wind.

She nodded.

"Your last official match."

"For now."

He reached down, took her hand, and traced a circle across the inside of her palm.

"You ever regret stepping out of it?" he asked. "The matching?"

She looked around—the children laughing, the quiet between them, the way everything felt stitched together by years of hope and hesitation and, finally, grace.

"No," she said. "I regret not stepping into this sooner."

He pressed a kiss to her temple, said nothing.

The breeze carried the scent of mint and turned soil. A hawk circled high above the field, wings stretched wide against the dimming sky.

Esther exhaled slowly.

She was still learning peace. Still learning how to want, how to stay, how to believe she didn't need to earn what had already been given.

But in that moment—with his hand in hers and her name no longer a question on someone else's lips—she felt something settle.

Not perfect. Not finished.

But *real.*

And for the first time in a life spent building love for others, she knew she'd found her own.

THE END

www.ingramcontent.com/pod-product-compliance
Lightning Source LLC
La Vergne TN
LVHW041615220725
816782LV00009B/189
* 9 7 9 8 2 3 0 0 0 9 3 5 1 *